ONO THE TICKBIRD

Adapted by Melissa Lagonegro
from the script "Ono the Tickbird," written by Elise Allen
for the series developed for television by Ford Riley

Illustrated by Francesco Legramandi and Gabriella Matta

A GOLDEN BOOK • NEW YORK

Copyright © 2018 Disney Enterprises, Inc. All rights reserved. Published in the
United States by Golden Books, an imprint of Random House Children's Books, a division
of Penguin Random House LLC, 1745 Broadway, New York, NY 10019, and in Canada by
Penguin Random House Canada Limited, Toronto, in conjunction with Disney Enterprises, Inc.
Golden Books, A Golden Book, A Little Golden Book, the G colophon, and the distinctive
gold spine are registered trademarks of Penguin Random House LLC.

rhcbooks.com
ISBN 978-0-7364-3838-4 (trade) — ISBN 978-0-7364-3839-1 (ebook)
Printed in the United States of America

10 9 8 7 6 5 4 3 2 1

Kion, Fuli, Beshte, Ono, and Bunga patrol the grassy plains of the Pride Lands. They can't believe their eyes—trees are broken and roots are pulled up everywhere! A rhino has run through and destroyed everything in his path.

"What a mess!" exclaims Beshte the hippo.

The Lion Guard races off to stop the rhino from causing more damage, but they are too late. The rhino's horn is stuck in a baboons' tree! Baboons fly through the air with every shake of his head as he tries to get his horn loose. The rhino's name is Kifaru, and he needs help! The Lion Guard works together to free him.

"What's going on, Kifaru?" asks Kion. "Why are you causing so much trouble?"

"What trouble?" asks Kifaru, confused. He turns and nearly steps on Bunga. He takes another step and almost pokes Fuli with his horn. He turns again and just misses running into another tree! Kifaru can't see where he's going!

Rhinos have bad eyesight—but Kifaru's is *really* bad!

Just then, Ono notices something. "Kifaru doesn't have his tickbird!"

Tickbirds and rhinos are great partners. The tickbirds ride on the rhinos and warn them of danger they can't see. Then the tickbirds get to eat the ticks and other bugs off their rhinos' backs.

Kifaru is sad. His tickbird, Mwenzi, flew away and left him.
He needs his tickbird to help him get safely to Lake Matope.
That's where all the rhinos go to have fun in the mud.

Kion is determined to help Kifaru get to Lake Matope. "We need to find Mwenzi and ask him to come back!" declares the lion.

Bunga offers to guide Kifaru until they find Mwenzi. But the honey badger becomes so busy eating bugs off Kifaru's back that he forgets to tell Kifaru where to go. The rhino is heading straight for a cliff!

"Kifaru, stop!" shouts Ono. Luckily, Kifaru hears
him and stops just inches before falling off the cliff.
Everyone thinks Ono would make a great tickbird—
everyone except Ono. He'd much rather help the
Lion Guard find Mwenzi, but he reluctantly agrees
to help Kifaru.

Fuli the cheetah picks up Mwenzi's scent! Kion, Beshte, and Bunga join her as she follows the trail.

Ono hops on Kifaru's back, ready to guide him. He tells the rhino to go in one direction, but Kifaru goes the opposite way.

"This is going to be a *loooong* trip," says Ono with a sigh.

The others have been looking for Mwenzi for a long time without much luck.

"I think I've seen this tree before," says Beshte.

"You have," replies Fuli, frustrated. "We're just going in circles!"

Meanwhile, Ono is also frustrated, riding on Kifaru's back. Kifaru snorts and makes loud noises. He never listens to Ono's directions. He makes Ono scratch his itches. And he constantly compares Ono to Mwenzi!

Kion and the others finally find Mwenzi! They try to convince the tickbird that his rhino needs him, but Mwenzi is mad at Kifaru.

"Just come with us and talk to him," pleads Beshte. "Real friends work things out."

"You think he misses me?" asks a hopeful Mwenzi.

"Of course he does!" replies the hippo.

Mwenzi agrees to talk to Kifaru. The Lion Guard sighs with relief.

Back on the path to Lake Matope, Kifaru continues to be difficult. Ono just can't seem to make him happy like Mwenzi did.

"If you weren't so bad at being a tickbird, I'd never know how wonderful Mwenzi really is!" exclaims Kifaru. He realizes how much he misses his friend.

Kifaru plops down on the ground. He's overheated and has to cool off. Ono flaps his big wings, creating a breeze.

"Oh, this is nice!" says Kifaru happily. Ono is finally doing something right!

Just then, the Lion Guard arrives with Mwenzi. The tickbird sees that Kifaru is happy with Ono and feels jealous.

"Kifaru!" shouts Mwenzi, annoyed.

"Mwenzi! You came back!" exclaims the rhino. He shoves Ono out of the way.

Mwenzi flies off, angrier than before. Ono zooms after him.

Ono finds Mwenzi sitting on a branch dangling over
a swamp filled with crocodiles. He tells Mwenzi what a
great tickbird he is and how much Kifaru needs him.

"He drives me crazy, but he is my best friend,"
Mwenzi admits. He agrees to be Kifaru's tickbird again.

Suddenly, Makuu, a crocodile, hits Mwenzi with his tail. The tickbird tumbles toward Makuu's open mouth, but Ono grabs him just in time!

Mwenzi's wing is hurt and he can't fly. Ono gently puts him high in a tree and races to get help.

Ono finds Kifaru and the Lion Guard. He tells them that Mwenzi is in trouble. Kifaru runs through the savannah to save his friend. The Lion Guard follows.

Kifaru and the Lion Guard fight off Makuu and the other crocodiles. From up in the tree, Mwenzi helps. Listening to his tickbird's directions, Kifaru swings a tree trunk with his horn and knocks the crocodiles far away. He saves Mwenzi *and* the Lion Guard!

"That's what you get when you mess with my best friend!" yells Kifaru.

"Great job, guys. Thanks!" says Kion.

"I couldn't have done it without my tickbird," says Kifaru, smiling at Mwenzi.

"And I couldn't have done it without my rhino," replies Mwenzi.

Kifaru and Mwenzi make it to Lake Matope together.

"Looks like they're having fun," says Kion.

"It must be nice to have a great friend with you all the time," declares Beshte.

"Yeah!" exclaims Bunga. "Hey, Ono! Wanna be *my* tickbird?"

"I'll always be your friend, Bunga. But my tickbird days are over," says Ono with a laugh.